GONE

NELL BRACH, PREQUEL

S. E. GREEN

Copyright © S. E. Green, 2024

The right of S. E. Green to be identified as the author of this work has been asserted per the Copyright, Designs and Patents Act 1976. All rights reserved. No part of this publication may be reproduced, transmitted, or stored in a retrieval system, in any form or by any means, without permission in writing from the publisher, nor be otherwise circulated in any form of binding or cover other than that in which it is published and without a similar condition being imposed on the subsequent purchaser. All characters in this publication are fictitious and any resemblance to real people, alive or dead, is purely coincidental.

PROLOGUE

A deer hops through knee-high grass, not far from me and Grandpa. We're camouflaged, hunting rifles in hand. I glance over to my favorite person in the world. Grandpa's a serious man, imposing, still built like the Army Ranger he used to be before becoming a cop, then sheriff. He doesn't move a muscle. He wants me to take the shot.

I go back to looking at the deer.

With a slow breath out, I sight it, then pull the trigger. The animal stumbles shot clean in the head and collapses.

A silent moment ticks by.

As Grandpa quietly prays, my lips move to the words I've heard him speak countless times. "Grant us wisdom and respect to keep us humble. Embrace this animal's spirit and bless this gift of nourishment to our family. May we keep this memory forever so that every time we hunt, we remember and honor this animal."

"Amen," I whisper.

Still crouched in our blind, Grandpa looks at me through the early morning mist. "I'm proud of you, Nell."

"Thank you, Grandpa."

"I want you to listen closely to my words." He pauses, allowing time for his gaze to penetrate mine. "You listening?"

"Yes, sir."

"Always be ready. No matter what. You don't know what's going to happen in this world. *You* are the only person you can rely on. You've got to be ready to do what's needed to protect those you love. Your mom, she's just like your grandmother, a fragile woman. And your little brother needs a strong person watching out for him. That's you." His brown eyes narrow. "You hear me?"

I nod.

Grandpa keeps looking at me like he wants to say more or perhaps he's not satisfied that I heard him. I'm about to assure him when he stands up and walks away from me toward the deer.

I couldn't know that would be my last weekend with him.

ONE

Six Months Later

An old station wagon covered in bumper stickers passes us as we pull into our new neighborhood. "New" is a generous word. Like the rest of White Quail, Tennessee, its best days are far behind.

I steer our '65 Chevy short bed along Shadow Lane, creeping past postage-sized brick homes with slush-covered lawns. Up ahead, I spy Grandpa's house, and just the sight of it brings me peace. Between that house, this truck, and the contents within, it's all we have left of him.

Beside me sits Tyler, my six-year-old brother. On the other side of him is Mom. She sighs heavy and deep, and her voice comes thin. "Never thought I'd be moving back into my old home."

"I love it here," I say.

Tyler arches up, trying to see over the dash. "What are we going to do first?"

"Eat," Mom and I say in unison, and then share a smile.

The front door opens as I park the truck. Mom's longtime best friend, Olivia, appears. Smiling, she waves. Her six-year-old son, Luca, pushes past, running out. Before I get the driver's door open, Tyler's shoving at me to get out. He's excited to see Luca. As they squeal and jump around, Mom and Olivia share a sweet and welcoming hug. I hope being around Olivia will cheer Mom up.

Moving here from Georgia is a good decision. Mom will see that. Other than the apartment we rented, Mom's job at Popeye's, and my job cleaning homes, we had nothing. Here we'll have an actual house that's paid for, I'll start the police academy soon, and Olivia already set Mom up with a data entry job where she'll work from home and have more time for Tyler.

Finally, we'll get ahead.

"The place is all cleaned and ready. Grace helped me bring food over. Your boxes arrived yesterday. Thought we'd eat and then help you unpack." Olivia comes around the truck to hug me next. "Lord, you're tall."

"You saw me six months ago. I haven't grown."

She feels my bicep. "Your mom said you've been working out."

"Getting ready for the academy." Grabbing my wallet and keys from the dash, I ask, "Is Grace here?"

"Inside." Olivia throws an arm around me and together we make our way into Mom's childhood home.

"DID you get here by taking the double-secret passthrough?" Tyler asks Luca.

"You know it." Luca crams a miniature brownie into his mouth.

The "double-secret pass-through" is just a path through the trees that connects our neighborhood to the one beside us where Olivia lives. Every few weeks, Grandpa used to take his sheers and cut back rogue branches and weeds. Now that he's gone, I suppose I'll do that for the two neighborhoods.

Grace plops down beside me on Grandpa's brown plaid couch. To her mom, she says, "I found a car. It's two thousand. Do you think you can kick in some money? I can't keep borrowing your car and as much as I love Matthew, it's not his job to chauffeur me."

Olivia sighs. "I sure am going to try. You know I'm doing my best."

"I know." Grace picks at the loose hem of her sweatshirt. "I wish we could sell that stupid studio."

"You and me both," Olivia agrees.

I bump my shoulder against Grace's, letting her know I get it. We've spent our entire lives not having money. Her dad died five years ago, leaving them with a run-down recording studio that eventually ran its course. Now the building sits empty and hosts a family of rodents and more than one spider.

"Speaking of used cars, I need one. We opted to sell mine. It wouldn't have made the trip here anyway." Mom comes from the kitchen, carrying two glasses of blush wine. She hands one to Olivia before sitting in a rocking chair near the empty fireplace. "You make that mac and cheese or did you buy it and plate it like a faker?"

Olivia laughs. "Plate it like a faker, of course. And we can go look at cars next week if you want."

"Sounds great." Taking a sip, Mom eyes Grace over the

rim. "You, my dear, get more and more gorgeous every time I see you."

Grace accepts the compliment with an awkward and shy smile, but it is the truth. Mom's not just being nice. Grace is beautiful.

"Now that you have your associates, what are you thinking about?" Mom asks. "You going for your bachelors?"

Grace hesitates. "Um, probably not. I might have a secretary job at the elementary school. I go in for a second interview soon."

"Here's hoping then." Mom smiles.

"When do you start your training?" Grace looks at me. "First of the year, right?"

"Yes, I can't wait."

"Following in her grandpa's footsteps," Mom mumbles.

She doesn't like that I want to be a cop. She was raised by one. I get it. But I've never wanted to do anything else. I'd planned on joining the force back in Georgia, but then Grandpa passed and here we are.

Done with their brownies and bored with us, Tyler and Luca jump up from the living room floor. "Can we go outside and play?"

"Stay in sight," Olivia says.

I stand up, pulling Grace with me and shooing the boys. "Get your jackets, your hats, gloves, scarves, and whatever else, and let's go."

OUTSIDE, the boys race around the yard singing, "Great green gobs of greasy, grimy gopher guts..."

Grace and I sit on the broken-down porch, idly watching.

"That is the grossest song," she says.

"Which is exactly why they sing it."

"Boys."

We share a smile.

"So, is it weird being in the house?" Grace asks.

"A little." Six months ago, Grandpa suffered a heart attack and died. I was here visiting over a long weekend when it happened. He came home one night from being out with a friend. Something seemed off about him. But when I asked, he simply shooed me off and went to bed.

I found him the next morning.

At least he went in his sleep, Mom had said.

I guess, but it bothers me how unaffected she seems by the whole thing.

"Talk to your dad recently?" Grace asks next.

"Of course not." I shrug. "I hate it for Tyler more than anything. He's been asking about Dad a lot."

"What do you tell him?"

"I tell him the truth. That Dad never wanted a family. Mom, though, keeps his hopes up. 'Your dad will come around. Just wait and see.' Drives me nuts when she tells him that. There's a reason he never married her. There's a reason he insisted we didn't take his last name. Mom's always been his one reliable booty call."

"I'm sorry."

"Yeah, me, too."

Tucking her bare hands into the pockets of her jean jacket, Grace leans in. "Now that we're alone." Excitement dances through her eyes. "Matthew proposed."

"Get out!"

She laughs. "I said yes, of course."

I hug her. "Oh, Grace, I'm so happy for you." Marrying

Matthew and having his babies is all she has wanted since the moment they met back in ninth grade.

"We're telling Mom together, so keep it quiet for now."

"For sure. Olivia loves Matthew. She's going to be thrilled."

"I know!"

An old station wagon pulls into the neighborhood, circling slowly through the houses. Bumper stickers cover every inch. I saw that earlier when we first arrived. I watch it, expecting it to park at a house, but instead, it keeps weaving through the neighborhood, eventually rolling past our house.

The boys see it and start dancing and singing, "Great green gobs of greasy grimy gofer guts..." They turn around and pretend to moon the station wagon.

"Boys!" Grace yells. "Absolutely not!" She stands up, waving to the station wagon. "Sorry about that!"

The wagon drives past, its windows cracked, the smell of pot filtering out. I see the faint image of a bald man driving. I note it's license plate as I watch it leave the neighborhood. "You seen that car before?" I ask.

"No, can't say I have."

BACK IN GRANDPA'S HOME, dirty dishes pile the counter that separates the kitchen from the living room where Grace and I are currently washing up. Mom and Olivia finish off their second bottle of wine. Their inebriated laughter brings a smile to my face.

Tyler and Luca race into the living room, both dressed to go outside.

"Stay where we can see you," I tell them and they squeal as they run out.

Grace eyes our drunk moms. "Good thing neither of them has to work tomorrow."

"Good thing." I glance out the front windows, seeing the boys chase each other.

Grace makes a pot of coffee. "When do you think our moms have reached their limit?"

"When they pass out."

We both laugh.

I keep washing and Grace dries. Grandpa didn't believe in dishwashers. Well, I do, and when I get some money saved, I'm buying us one.

Another glance out the front window shows the boys now sword fighting with sticks.

Grace snaps the lid onto the leftover potato salad before sliding it into the refrigerator. Olivia and Mom start singing a *Bon Jovi* song.

"Guess we're unpacking tomorrow," I say, eyeing our mellow moms.

Grace chuckles. "Yep. Maybe we can do Christmas decorations, too."

"That sounds fun." Smiling, I look again out the window...

But the boys are gone.

I cross over to the front door. An empty yard greets me. "Tyler! Luca!"

"What's going on?" Grace calls from the kitchen.

Outside, I look up the street and down. "Tyler! Luca!"

"Nell?" Mom says.

A quick jog around the house shows nothing. Back inside, I'm greeted with three pairs of concerned eyes. "The boys are gone." I race down the hall, Grace on my heels, checking every room and closet. Both moms are on their feet when I return to the living room.

Grace shoves her arms into her jean jacket and hands me my bomber one. "Come on. Luca probably took Tyler to our house."

We take off running, cutting around Grandpa's lot. We cross our neighbor's backyard and duck through the pass-through over to their neighborhood. Their house sits four down on the right.

Grace has the key out and ready and lets us in. Their house looks a lot like ours with three bedrooms, one bath, a kitchen, and a living room. An attached garage is the only difference.

Splitting up, we move fast, checking each room and closet, calling out, "Tyler? Luca?" We double-time it, looking under beds, and meet up at the garage.

She flicks on the light to show a space full of surplus toilet paper, canned goods, and boxed food. "Boys?" she yells.

"They're not here."

"Maybe they're in your grandfather's shed."

That's not likely. No one goes inside Grandpa's shed. Still, though, we waste no time backtracking their neighborhood over to ours. We run into our moms.

"Anything?" my mom asks.

"No." Breathing heavily, I push past her, running to the shed. I note the usual sturdy lock securing the doors. I yank at it anyway.

"What's in there?" Grace asks.

"I think just Grandpa's tools and hunting supplies."

"Oh, God," Olivia mutters.

"I don't believe this." Mom turns a circle. "How can they not be in either place?"

"The station wagon!" I grab Grace's arm.

"What station wagon?" Olivia asks.

"It had bumper stickers all over it. They pretended to moon it," Grace says. "It drove by earlier."

"Call 911!" Mom screams.

I write down the license number that I memorized and give it to Grace. As Olivia calls nine-one-one, I jump in Grandpa's truck and slam it into reverse.

I will find that station wagon.

TWO

I'm not sure how long I drive in and out of neighborhoods, up and down roads, and back and forth through town. But it must be hours because day transitions to night and sleet begins to fall.

My phone rings. It's mom. "Anything?" I ask.

"No," she whispers. "The cops are looking for that station wagon."

"It's a small town. How in the hell do they not know a station wagon with bumper stickers all over it? Jesus Christ."

"Where are you?"

"I'm about to get on the interstate. I searched every corner of town." On the dash, the gas light flashes red. Up ahead near the entrance to I-81 I spy an empty station with two pumps and a small building that houses the attendant. "I'm getting gas," I say as I pull in. "I'll call you if I—" Darkness cloaks the back side of the parking lot, but still, I see it —a vehicle facing thick woods.

"What is it?"

"Mom, it's here. The station wagon is here. Call the cops." I rattle off the location and hang up.

From the glove box, I grab the full-size metal flashlight and from under the driver's seat, I find the hunting knife Grandpa gave me.

With both in hand, I throw open the driver's door. My phone rings again, but I ignore it, sprinting past the attendant.

My pace slows as I approach the rear of the station wagon. I'm about to flick on my light when the engine roars to life. Oh hell, no. I unsheathe the hunting knife and jab it hard, twice, into the back wheel.

Air hisses out.

The driver's door flings open and with it a cloud of smoke barrels out, reeking of marijuana. Turning on my flashlight, I direct the beam. A frail man with a bald head squints at me. "Why'd you do that?" he asks.

"Get out of the car!"

He blinks, but he doesn't move.

With the light still blinding him, I move alongside the station wagon and try the handle of the back door. It opens to a seat covered in fast-food wrappers.

The man coughs.

"Where are they?" I move to the rear hatch, trying the handle and finding it unlocked too. Carpet spans the interior with piles of clothes. From this angle, I have a clear shot of the entire station wagon. The boys aren't here.

I shine my light past the wagon and into the woods. "Tyler? Luca?" I call out.

The man coughs again, bringing up phlegm.

"Is that why you're here? Did you put them in the woods?" I slam the hatch and round the car back to the driver's side. "I said get out of the car."

Still, he doesn't move.

Grabbing the neck of his jacket, I drag him out of the seat. He trips and lands face down on the wet pavement.

The beam of my flashlight sweeps the edge of the woods, illuminating a slurry of leaves and slushy mud. "Tyler!" I scream. "Luca."

The man groans. "Why are you yelling?"

I come down next to him. Lifting his head, I put my hunting knife right in front of his eyes. "I swear to God, I will cut you. Where is my brother?"

He doesn't respond. He's completely fried.

"What's going on?"

Turning, I see an old groggy man with a gray bedhead. He stands dressed in overalls and backlit by the flickering florescent light coming from the two pumps. His bloodshot eyes move from me to the station wagon and then over to the man still lying face down.

The groggy guy takes a hesitant step back. Sirens pierce the air and blue lights flash.

Sheathing my knife and tucking it away, I stand up just as two cop cars catch the three of us in their lights.

ONE OF THE cops hauls the driver of the station wagon off the ground. He pushes him up against the vehicle. "What is your name?"

The man thinks about that question entirely too long. "Carl Kemp."

Shining a light in his face, the cop studies him. I stand several yards away, really getting a good look at him now. He looks to be seventy-something years old.

Blankly, he stares into the flashlight beam.

"Where are the two little boys?" the cop demands.

"I don't know." He smacks his lips. "Can I have something to drink?" Carl looks past the beam and over to me. "She punctured my tire. Why did she do that?"

"Because you were about to leave, you asshole."

The second cop approaches. "The car's registered to Donna Kemp. Is that your wife?"

Carl doesn't answer.

"Driving under the influence." The first cop turns Carl face-first against the wagon, and, as he reads him his rights, he places him in handcuffs.

Cop number two calls things in. The groggy gas attendant man goes back to his small building. And I cross back over to Grandpa's truck.

Carl and Donna Kemp.

Their house shouldn't be hard to find.

THE KEMPS live out in the country in the next county over. Google Maps takes me down a long road, then a short one that cuts along a landfill, ending at several acres of unkempt land with a double-wide, dingy-yellow trailer surrounded by woods.

Up on a hill to the left and tucked into thick trees sits a weathered home, dark and deserted.

There are no lights this far out in the country. I struggle to see. The whole area depresses me.

Once upon a time, this place might have been nice, but not now. A light coming from within tells me someone's home. It's one of those places that's so far out and isolated, that no one would hear if someone screamed.

That thought does not sit well with me.

I pull down the short driveway and park.

My shoes sink into the muddy yard as I cross over to the front door.

A sixty-something-year-old woman opens it before I knock. She wears a burgundy shawl that she wraps around her shoulders against the cold. With long silver and black hair curled away from her face, she has a regal air to her that doesn't match Carl.

"May I help you?"

"Ma'am, my name is Nell Brach. I'm looking for my little brother and his friend. Their names are Tyler and Luca." I pull Tyler's photo up on my phone and show it to her. "Have you seen him?"

She studies the photo. "No."

"Carl Kemp is your husband?"

She doesn't seem surprised by the question as she opens the door and invites me in. "It's cold. Let's talk in here."

After wiping my shoes, I walk into a small living room cramped with old furniture. A cat is asleep on a frayed couch. She sits beside the cat, nodding for me to take a wood-backed chair directly across from her.

The room is warm, musty, and filled only by the ticking of a clock. I want to take my jacket off, but I don't.

"Carl's a good man," she says. "He got some bad news recently and has been a bit off." On the table next to her sits a framed photo of the two of them at a much younger age, grinning for the camera. Beside that is a framed photo of a teenage boy and another of a man in his thirties.

"Your children?" I ask.

"Junior and Harry. Junior's the oldest. He committed suicide about ten years ago now. Always a troubled boy, that Junior. Harry was our late in life baby. Thought I was in menopause and turned up pregnant. Anyway, he's been gone a year. Hunting accident."

"That's a lot of loss for one family. I'm sorry," I say.

She accepts the sentiment with a nod.

I look around the overly-decorated, outdated room. "Ma'am, have you already talked to the cops?"

"I have. Yes. They were just here. I gave them full access to search every nook and cranny. I've got—*we've* got—nothing to hide."

Well, that explains her lack of shock over all of this.

"Can I ask what bad news your husband recently received?"

"Cancer diagnosis. He doesn't have long to live."

My phone buzzes with a call from Grace. "I need to take this. Thank you for your time." I see myself out as I answer the call. "What do you know?"

"They're putting together a search party," she tells me. "In the woods that surround that gas station where you found the wagon. Meet you there?"

"Yes."

COPS AND VOLUNTEERS swarm the gas station's lot. Wearing orange vests, people head off into the woods. Flashlight beams move through the night.

Grace catches sight of me and waves me over to park next to a beat-up Jeep. Her fiancé, Matthew, is with her. They're both already dressed in orange vests and holding flashlights.

On the seat beside me is the full-sized metal one I used before. I grab it and meet them by the Jeep.

Matthew offers me a firm and warm hug. He looks

exactly like he did when I was here six months ago—big, strong, and reliable. "I'm so sorry this is happening, Nell."

"Thank you." I take the orange vest Grace hands me. "Where's Olivia and my mom?"

"They stayed back, each in one house, in case the boys return."

With a nod, I flick on my light and step into the woods. "Let's go."

The three of us spread out, joining the rest. With measured and cautious steps, we begin scanning the ground...

THREE

With the woods combed and nothing found, and with dawn having moved in, the search party dissipates.

Exhausted, I follow Grace and Matthew home. They pass Grandpa's neighborhood, going one turn down to Grace's house.

The sheriff's car sits in our driveway, the bottom half covered in sludge. I park the truck in our yard, giving the sheriff room to leave.

Down the street I see a few neighbors out, dressed in thick clothes, drinking morning coffee and gossiping. They look up at me and sober.

In the house, I take my muddy shoes off and bomber jacket, leaving both by the front door. I find Mom and Sheriff Owens sitting at Grandpa's round kitchen table.

Sheriff Owens took over when my grandpa died. I've only met him once, at Grandpa's memorial service. With light brown hair and clean-shaven, he's my mom's age. Grandpa didn't care for Owens. *Cocky son of a bitch*, he said more than once.

"It's nice to see you again, Nell." Owens extends a hand that I shake. "Jill and I were just talking through things."

My mom and the sheriff went to high school together. According to Mom, back then he was super popular and Mr. Athlete. He and my mom didn't run in the same circles.

I turn to her, finding her eyes closed and her head back, looking more exhausted than I feel.

A carafe of coffee sits in the center of the table with a box of donuts beside it, uneaten. I help myself to a glazed one and pour a mug from the carafe before sliding into the chair beside Mom. I take a sip, finding it stale and cool. I don't care. I take another drink, followed by a bite of donut.

"What do we know?" I ask Sheriff Owens.

"As you know, Carl Kemp was arrested for driving under the influence. Our lab tech found nothing in the station wagon. It was filthy, but none of that filth belonged to the boys."

Somehow this news doesn't surprise me. "They were wearing hats and gloves, likely leaving no hair or prints to collect."

He smiles a little. "Our legacy enrollment. I'm looking forward to working with you after you graduate."

"Thank you. I'm set to start the academy after the New Year."

With a nod, he continues, "We also searched the Kemp home, finding nothing. Nell, I know you went out to see Donna Kemp. It's important that you not get involved in this investigation. It could ruin things in court when the time comes."

Opening her eyes, Mom lifts her head. She drinks coffee, not speaking. I hand her a donut, but she shakes her head. Despite the worn-out shock in her expression, she's composed. Doggedly so. Photos scatter the kitchen table, mostly of Tyler, but some of Luca.

Picking one up, she hands it to Sheriff Owens. "Use this one."

He takes the picture.

Mom's eyes fill with tears. Just seeing hers makes my eyes heat, too. But I can't cry. If I do, I won't stop.

Outside, the faint sound of a garbage truck circles the neighborhood. The backup beeping drifts into our house.

Humbly, Sheriff Owens looks at me, showing none of the cockiness Grandpa complained about. His words come with unwavering conviction. "I will exhaust every avenue to find your brother."

"How long are you keeping Carl?"

"Now that he's sobered up, I'm heading back to the station to question him. Nell, the man is dying of cancer."

"So?"

"I'm just saying. They've also lost two sons. It's not been easy for them." The sheriff's voice comes calm. "No one is crossed off the list yet. Let me do my job, okay? I'm good at it. I'm going to repeat what I said a moment ago, it is important that you not get involved in the investigation." The sheriff stands. "Now, time for me to have that talk with Carl." With that, he walks out.

FOUR

Twenty-four hours missing and Sheriff Owens has exactly shit.

Has he even bothered to check the sex offenders in the area? Because I'm looking at the list right now.

There are three who live within a ten-mile radius of Grandpa's home.

The first one is 59, muscled, and wearing workout clothes when he answers the door.

"Sir, my name is Nell Brach and I'm looking for my younger brother, Tyler." I show him a photo on my phone. "Have you seen him?"

"No." The man sighs, but he doesn't seem annoyed. "What I did was a very long time ago. And consensual. I paid my dues."

A woman steps up beside him, a toddler on her hip. "What's going on?"

I repeat myself, showing her the photo.

"We don't know anything about this. You are welcome to come into our home and look around. We have nothing to hide. My husband is a good man. What we did when I was sixteen and he was twenty was consensual. My father should have never brought charges against him. We've been married thirty years now. We have three children and two grandchildren. When will this all blow over?"

I back away. "My apologies."

THE SECOND IS 27, skinny, and works as a fry cook at Waffle House.

He's shaking his head before I finish telling him who I am.

"I know about the missing boys," he says. "I've got nothing to do with it. I was working when they went missing. Ask anyone in this place. Plus, I would never touch a little boy."

Yeah, but you'll touch a little girl, I want to say but don't.

"He's telling the truth," an acne-scarred waitress says. "We worked a double yesterday. And we're rolling into another one tonight.

THE THIRD IS 66 and a former school teacher.

My headlights wash over a cheaply built gray house with a flickering light on inside. I park Grandpa's truck behind one just as old as his. With a check of my notes to make sure I'm at the correct address, I down the last of the coffee I bought and open the driver's door.

Icy air drifts along my neck, and shivering, I cross over the shabby yard. One step up takes me to the front door. A cracked bell produces no sound. Exhaustion moves over me, pissing me off. I don't have time to be tired.

I knock hard, yelling, "Hello?"

The door opens. Sheriff Owens greets me with a scowl. Behind him, a gray-haired man in a wheelchair gives me a once over.

Sheriff Owens comes from the house, closing the door behind him. "Turn around. I'm following you home."

FIVE

Sure enough, Sheriff Owens follows me home. He should be scouring the planet and instead he's acting like my babysitter.

In our front yard he gives me a disciplinary look. "You are wasting my time. I cannot do my job if I'm looking over my shoulder for you. I should not have to escort you home. Do you want me to post a cop in your yard? Because I will."

"No."

"Then go inside and be with your mother."

"What did Carl say? Why was he in this neighborhood?"

"He's buying a house in the area. That's why he drove by your place. Now, go inside."

"A man dying of cancer is buying a house? That's bullshit."

"Go inside."

"Did you let him go?"

Sheriff Owens takes a patient breath. "Why are you sure Carl's involved, other than the station wagon driving through your neighborhood?"

My hands shake. I ball them into fists. The sheriff notes the movement. I look him in the eye. "Grandpa told me to always trust my gut. And my gut says Carl Kemp is involved. Did you let him go?"

"Yes, Carl Kemp has been released but under instructions that he won't leave the area. Nell, he's scheduled for chemotherapy today. The man is dying."

"As you've already said."

INSIDE, I find Mom curled up on the bed, hysterically sobbing, with Grace holding on to her. Manic terror fills the air. For a desperate second, I fear they've heard the worst. But then I remember I was just with the sheriff. He would've told me.

Grace looks at me through destitute, freaked-out eyes. I recognize that look. I know that look. She's found Mom this way.

"Oh, God, why hasn't he come home?" Mom cries. "It's been two days." She clings to Grace. "Make him come home. I don't understand. Make him come home."

Motioning Grace to get up, I take her place. I hold Mom while she cries. Grace stands awkwardly in the doorway, watching.

For long moments, Mom weeps. It's all I can do to hold her and control my own tears.

Eventually, she pulls back. "You were supposed to be watching him."

My mouth opens. I start to answer, but nothing comes out. I feel sick with shame. She's right. I should've checked on them. I should've known.

"Just go," she says.

I turn away from her stare. My eyes meet Grace's, and hers tear up. I leave the bedroom and walk past my friend into the hallway. Leaning against the wall, I duck my head and take a second.

"She didn't mean it," Grace quietly says.

"Yes, she did." With a sigh, I look at her. "Where's your mom?"

"At home, staring at the phone."

"I'm heading back out. Can you handle both of our moms?"

Grace doesn't answer. Her gaze begs me not to leave. I hold her stare, and guilt festers inside of me—about the boys, about leaving Grace here to handle Mom, about Olivia over in her house, grieving too.

I hug my friend. "I'm scared, too."

Crying, she clings to me. We stand in the hallway, grieving for possible news to come but also in denial that this is our world now.

OUTSIDE, I sit in Grandpa's truck. But I don't turn the key. I don't do anything but stare at the front of our new home.

I was the one who insisted we come here.

I was the one who said we needed a fresh start.

I was the one who bugged Mom until she said yes.

Mom would have sold Grandpa's house, stayed in Georgia, and never come back to this town where she was raised.

We would be in Georgia right now, the three of us, safe and living our lives. If it wasn't for me.

Trouble, Nell. It's all we can expect in this world. It's

how we react to it that defines us. Are you going to roll over, or are you going to fight?

Grandpa's words come back to me, clouding my mind but also ringing true. My fingers hover over the ignition key. I want to go somewhere, anywhere, but where?

I crank the engine, then slam the gear shift into reverse. I know exactly where I'm going.

SIX

At the hospital, I locate Carl Kemp and I watch as he finishes up chemotherapy. From the late hour, it must be the last appointment of the day.

I follow at a careful distance when he walks through the hospital and out the doors.

At the front entrance, he texts someone before cutting around the side and onto the back where dumpsters sit. He keeps going, walking a short path to a park. Mature trees line the area, offering privacy. I'm sure in the daytime hospital staff come here for fresh air and lunch.

At night, though, the place sits empty.

One street light offers, at best, dim illumination.

I smell damp winter air—a sign of more sleet to come.

I'm not sure what I'm doing here. I guess I just wanted to see him.

He lights a joint.

Enough time goes by that the moon rises, hanging heavy and nearly full, but mostly blocked by winter storm clouds. Enough time goes by that Carl gets properly baked.

He looks up to the moon, inhaling and holding, then blowing out. As he blows out, he begins to softly sing.

Quietly, I move closer, straining to hear.

A breeze rolls past, carrying his slurred words, "Great green gobs of greasy grimy gopher guts. Swimming in—"

Beside me a fire ring is lined with big stones. I don't fully know what I'm doing as I lean down, pick one up, and step from the shadows.

HEADLIGHTS FLASH through the night as I pull into the abandoned studio that Grace's dad used to own but that now sits empty. I back in. In the rearview, I look at myself, recalling Grandpa's words.

You don't know what's going to happen in this world. You are the only person you can rely on. You've got to be ready to do what's needed to protect those you love. Your mom, she's just like your grandmother, a fragile woman. And your little brother needs a strong person watching out for him.

Would Grandpa be doing this? Yes, he would.

More determined now, I cut the engine, grab my flashlight, and get out.

In the back of the truck is one of his toolboxes. I find a crow bar and go about breaking the lock on the studio's back door.

I lower the tailgate.

Carl's there, passed out, covered in a tarp.

I put the tarp on the ground and pull Carl out of the truck's bed. With a thud, he lands on the tarp. I make quick work of retrieving duct tape from the toolbox, before dragging Carl through the studio's door and closing it behind me.

Pitch black surrounds me.

I flick on my flashlight.

The beam bounces off dust coating the floor and rodent droppings scattered about.

A narrow passage leads into what used to be a lounge. Cobwebs span the corners and stains drip the walls from a leaky roof.

The lounge moves into an office. Despite my racing pulse, I shiver.

A thick black door separates the office from the sound-proof studio.

I have a very clear and distinct memory of coming here with Grace when we were tiny girls. Her father had us record *Happy Birthday* for her mom. We giggled and danced and sang.

Now my memory will be of this.

The twenty-by-twenty-foot room is empty and dusty like the rest of the place. I drag Carl in.

It takes me a lot longer than expected to duct tape his arms and legs and body, like a mummy. Blood cakes the side of his head where I hit him with the rock. Between that and his cancer, he looks like death.

What if I'm wrong? snakes into my head, and I immediately shove it out. I'm not wrong. This man knows where Tyler and Luca are. I have to make him talk.

I heard him singing their song.

The boys are only six years old. They will die if I don't make this man talk.

With a groan, he slowly wakes.

I come down next to him. "Where are they?"

But Carl doesn't answer because he once again loses consciousness.

I NOW SIT on the floor, my back against the soundproof wall.

Wincing, I flex my hands open and they quiver when my fingers stretch wide. They've been clenched for the hour I've been here.

I crawl over to Carl, once again checking his pulse. I've done this several times over the past hour.

I go back to my spot, staring at him, silently willing him to wake up.

Beside me is a water bottle I retrieved from the truck some time ago. I unscrew the lid and pour it over his head.

It does nothing to stir him.

I either hit him too hard or he's just too high.

He wakes then, slowly, his eyes fluttering open. It takes him a second to realize he's duct taped and when he does he begins thrashing. He doesn't even know I'm here.

"Hey," I say.

He stops thrashing, rolling over to look at me.

"I have been sitting here staring at you wondering how far I will go to get what I want. I'd like to think I'm capable of torture, especially when it comes to my brother. But I don't know. I've never done that before."

Carl screams, loud and shrilling like he's a feral cat being strangled to death.

It makes me flinch.

I wait for him to stop, but he doesn't. So, I yell over him. "Go ahead, be as loud as you want! No one will hear. You're in a soundproof studio."

He keeps thrashing and screaming.

I walk from the room, closing the door. I stay still to listen, and sure enough, not a sound can be heard.

I'm about to walk back in when Grace texts me.

Grace: It's one in the morning. Where are you? Your mom is hysterical.

I want nothing more than to pretend I don't see the text, but that's not fair to Grace.

Me: I'm coming.

SEVEN

All the way home I think of the question: How far will I go to find Tyler? I will go all the way, without a doubt. I'm just not sure what that means exactly.

When I pull Grandpa's truck up into the driveway, Grace walks from my house, looking beyond exhausted.

I roll my window down. She says, "I'm going home. Your mom just now fell asleep."

"Thanks, Grace."

With a weary nod, she walks toward the gap in the trees that leads to her neighborhood.

Rolling my window back up, I cut the engine.

But I don't go in. Instead, I tuck my hands into the pockets of my bomber jacket and I close my eyes.

A POLITE KNOCKING on the driver's side window jolts me.

A woman about my age stands outside the truck, smiling, motioning me to roll the window down. It's light out. Frost covers the windshield and cold seeps into my bones.

I fell asleep.

Clearing my throat, I roll the window down. "Yes?"

"Hi. Are you the sister of the missing boy?"

"Are you a reporter?"

"Kind of. I do a podcast."

It's all I can do not to roll my eyes. "No comment."

"Wait, do you think your brother's disappearance has anything to do with the other little boy that went missing?"

"What other little boy?"

She points to the house right beside ours. "Ten years ago. You didn't know?"

I RUN INSIDE and grab a hot shower, followed by food. Before I leave, I check on Mom.

She's curled on her side, her back to the bedroom door.

"Mom?"

She doesn't stir.

I walk around the bed to find her eyes open. She doesn't look at me. "Do you need anything?" I quietly ask.

"No." She closes her eyes.

"I'm going to find him, Mom. I promise."

"Leave me alone."

THE HOUSE beside ours has new owners. It doesn't take me any time to find out the old owners and where they live now.

On the way to their house, I stop by a hardware store

and buy a new lock to replace the one I broke on the studio's back door.

As I walk through the interior of the run-down building, intermittent daylight filters in through boarded-up windows. It's enough I don't need my flashlight.

I enter what used to be the office, and a family of mice scatters.

I open the soundproof door. The smell of piss and sweat greets me.

Carl rolled across the room during the night, now in the corner, still duct-taped tight.

Other than his eyes that track my movements, he makes no sound or movement of his own.

I come down next to him, taking in his swollen jaw and the matted blood that covers a bruise spreading across his bald head. I hit him good with that rock. Twice.

"You ready to tell me where Tyler and Luca are?"

"You don't know who you're dealing with."

"Oh yeah, who am I dealing with?"

"Just wait."

"Wait for what? You're the one trussed up like a pig."

He chuckles, low and menacing. The sound crawls my skin.

"You willing to die here? Because that's what I'll do. I'll leave you here to rot and starve to death. I don't care."

"Silly, silly girl."

My fist takes on a life of its own. I punch him in the nose. It's the first time I've ever used my fist on someone.

Blood swells from both nostrils, bubbling with his breath. "Go ahead," he says, his voice low and gravely. "Kill me. I don't care. I'm dying anyway. One thing you need to know about me? I don't cave. Whatever it is you want me to say, I won't say it."

I throw another punch, catching it before it connects. His flinch satisfies me. I leave him there and go in search of Jason and Nancy McMillan, the previous owners of the house beside ours.

ONE HOUR later I pull up outside a two-story brick, colonial-style home. I park in front of the garage and follow a stone path up to the front door.

I ring the bell.

It emits an elegant tune.

Inside shadows shift as a person moves through the house. A woman answers. I'd place her in her early fifties. Other than the white slippers on her feet, she looks dressed for work in a pencil skirt and tucked-in blouse.

Her defined eyebrows arc up with efficient manners. "Yes?"

"Are you Nancy McMillan?"

"Yes, I am. May I help you?"

"My name is Nell Brach. I believe you used to own the home beside mine. My brother Tyler, and his friend, Luca, are missing."

She hesitates, looking me up and down. "I already talked to the sheriff."

"Would you be willing to talk to me? I won't take much of your time."

"Let me make a call to work and then we'll chat."

I NOW SIT on a floral-patterned couch with a mug of coffee cradled in my hands.

Nancy is diagonal to me on a dark-framed chair upholstered in blush pink. "I swear that house is cursed. It's been in my family forever. My father lived there. Died there, too. Jason and I lived there as newlyweds. It's where I miscarried our first child during the third trimester. Eventually, we made the place into a rental property. The second person we rented to left something on the stove and caught the house on fire. The fourth person we rented to fell from the attic and broke her leg. There were months with no renters, but a burglar broke in, vandalized, and took what he could. Then came Randy, our son."

A look of pain crosses her face. She takes a moment to drink coffee and gather her thoughts. "Jason and I were over there after the break-in, putting things back together, painting walls, and what not. Randy was four. We had the front door open. Jason was in the back of the house. Randy was right there at the entryway. He'd just thrown a giant temper tantrum and was in time out. I ran to the bathroom, and when I came back, he was gone." She swallows. "Just like that. Gone."

The pain on her face transitions to a strange look, almost like she's insulted. "Jason wanted to blame me. Said I wasn't keeping a good enough watch. But I was, I promise you that. I was only gone a minute, maybe not even that."

I nod. "Believe me, I know."

"It's been nearly eleven years but I think about it every single day." Her voice distorts with fresh emotion. She looks away, her face deteriorating as she works hard to compose herself. "Christ." She grabs a tissue from a nearby canister and presses it into her eyes. "I thought I'd worn this reaction out. Every day we looked for him. The whole town did. We put up a reward. But nothing."

With the tissue now crumbled in her hand, she gazes at

me through unblinking eyes. "Nothing. This past year we finally sold the house. He'd be fifteen now."

Nervous energy has me wanting to pace, but my body stays where it is.

"To this day, no one can tell me what happened. No one saw anything. I don't know if Randy is dead or alive."

"No leads?"

"None."

A quiet moment goes by. She releases a breath, shaking her head and standing. She holds her back straight, unforgiving, but her voice quivers when she says, "Unfortunately, I can't help you. I can't go through this again. I know how valuable time is. You should go."

"Yes, ma'am." I place my mug on a coaster and I stand. "I appreciate you talking with me."

A framed photo of a little boy catches my eye. With light brown hair and freckles, he grins for the camera. "Is that Randy?"

"Yes."

"May I take a picture of that?"

"That's fine."

She sees me out after that, standing on the front porch as I walk to Grandpa's truck. "I know that truck. And I just figured out that you're Sheriff Brach's granddaughter."

"Yes."

She lets out a chuckle that holds no humor. "Your grandfather and my dad hated each other. They were even in a fist fight once out in front of your house."

"A fist fight about what?"

"My dad caught your grandfather carrying on with some married woman."

"That's not possible."

"Oh, it happened. Every time your grandfather saw my

dad, he got more and more pissed about the whole thing. He didn't like Dad knowing his dirty little secret. Your grandfather was a mean man. He yelled at me one time because I was trimming that pass-through that connects the two neighborhoods. 'That's my job!' he yelled. 'Get away from there!' I mean, I was so shocked I ran. Granted, he'd been drinking but still. Yeah, but no one messed with him because he was the sheriff. He got away with way too much. Especially with your grandmother."

"What are you talking about?"

"Dad said he was nasty to her. Used to grab her and push her around. Used to cuss at her and threaten her. She locked him out one time and he sat in that truck with his rifle, seething. He didn't back down until my dad called the cops for help. Dad was truly scared your grandfather was going to shoot your grandmother. Soon after's when she took off and left your poor mom all alone with your grandfather. But what really gets me is that when Randy went missing, your grandfather did nothing."

I TRY to focus on this new information about Randy McMillan, but all I can think of is the last part of our conversation. Nancy has to be wrong. Grandpa was a good and kind, strong and fearless man. He never would have had an affair with another man's wife. And he certainly was not abusive to my grandmother.

I try dialing Mom, but she doesn't pick up.

It's around two in the afternoon when I pull into the rear of the studio. I find Carl in the same place he was in hours ago.

"Hello," he says.

The one-word greeting makes my teeth grind.

"Is this what you do? Take little boys? First Randy, then Tyler and Luca?"

Silence.

I charge over to the corner where I left my flashlight and I hurl it at him. It hits his head and bounces off.

Carl Kemp sneers.

I lose it.

I grab the flashlight and I attack.

I slug him in the chest, the shoulder, the neck, the knee cap, the thigh, the foot, the arm, the back, the head... "WHERE ARE THEY?" I keep hitting his duct-taped body over and over again, until sweat flings from my brow.

Breathing heavily, I brace my foot in the center of his chest and I stare down at his swollen jaw, puffy eyes, and fresh blood trickling from a slit I just made in his eyebrow.

"You just made a big mistake."

I hold up the flashlight. "You were singing their song. Your station wagon was in our neighborhood. I know it's you. What do you want with them? You're dying for God's sake! Where are they? Does your wife know? Should I bring her in here and beat her?"

"Sure, go ahead."

With a furious scream, I stalk from the room.

In the exterior area, I hammer the wall with my fist.

Through the gap in the open door, I hear him laughing.

Another furious scream erupts from me. I slam the door and leave.

EIGHT

I now sit in the truck back out at Donna Kemp's place. With binoculars I survey the rundown area, not focusing on the trailer, but instead everything else.

In her yard sits a rental car. Guess the cops still have the station wagon. Carefully, I scrutinize the overgrown front and side yards and the woods that bracket the back.

Has she reported Carl missing? I don't know but it seems as if I would have heard by now if she had.

If she hasn't reported him missing, then why? Maybe she thinks he skipped town and is covering for him.

Next, I search for a shed, a basement, a cellar—anywhere Carl might have stashed the boys—but I find nothing.

With a sigh, I lower the binoculars.

The tiny abandoned house catches my eye, up on a hill and overlooking the Kemp property. Boarded up tight, it doesn't look like anybody has lived there in decades.

Still, I grab Grandpa's crowbar and walk the short distance, going up the gravel incline and onto the unstable porch. I try the handle, finding it locked. I walk the perimeter of the house, noting each window covered in nailed boards.

"Tyler? Luca?"

My voice is met with the quiet.

Using the crowbar, I pry one board loose. Daylight filters in and I cup my hands to the window seeing a one-room empty shack with an old woven throw rug, a wooden ladder propped against a wall, and a wood burning stove.

"Can I help you?"

I turn to see Donna Kemp standing some distance away, wearing a long wool sweater. Like before, she comes across regal and composed.

"Who lives here?"

"No one. This place has long been abandoned." She smiles kindly. "Any luck with your brother?"

"Where's Carl?" I ask, though of course I know where he is.

"I don't know. He never came home. I let the sheriff know." She turns away and starts walking down the driveway. "I'm having tea. Would you like some?"

"No." I follow her down. "Aren't you worried about Carl?"

"Oh, heavens no. This isn't the first time he's gone somewhere without telling me. We're both very independent that way. I trust he'll be back when he's ready."

"But he's dying."

"Something I have come to terms with." She keeps walking across the road and back onto her property. I go to my truck and start the engine, watching her, but she doesn't look back once as she walks into her trailer and closes the door.

MY NEIGHBORHOOD IS alive with activity. News crews line the curbs, neighbors and others mill about outside in the cold, flowers and miscellaneous gifts gather in my yard. Through the trees, I see the same thing going on around Grace's house.

I park the truck behind a news van and walk past a reporter talking into a camera.

"...Police are asking that anyone with information please call the twenty-four-hour tip line."

The reporter keeps talking.

I scan the crowd. Somber faces look back at me as if waiting for me to speak. I don't recognize any of them.

I exhale, and my breath fogs the air.

One by one the neighbors turn away, going back in their homes or pretending to do something outside so they can continue lurking.

A tall figure catches my attention, standing alone, staring at our house.

I walk to him and as I draw closer, he turns to look at me. With dark brown hair, wide set eyes, and a beard, something about him seems familiar.

I stop right in front of him, surveying his face. I'd place him in his thirties. With an unreadable expression, he simply stares back.

"Do I know you?" I ask.

He shakes his head. Then he turns and walks off.

I follow.

He leaves my neighborhood, going through the pass-through and coming out the other side. He turns. Our eyes lock. Again, I experience the unnerving sensation that I know him, or I recognize him, or something about him is familiar.

A dirt bike sits against the curb. He puts on a helmet, kicks it to start, and calmly rides off.

There is no plate for me to memorize.

In my house, I find Mom sitting on the couch, staring at the TV, watching the reporter outside of our house.

"I'm only here for a second to check on you," I tell her. "Are you doing okay?"

She doesn't respond.

I want to ask her about Grandpa and the things Nancy McMillan said but now is not the time. Instead, I kiss her head, and I'm about to leave when she asks, "Where exactly do you go when you leave here?"

"Everywhere. I'm not giving up. I'll find him, Mom."

Darkly, she considers me. "You do what you have to. You hear me? If it brings Tyler home, do it."

NINE

At the studio I find Carl asleep in the corner, shivering.

Kneeling beside him, I push him. "Wake up."

His eyes flutter open.

I pull up the photo of four-year-old Randy that I took and I shove it in Carl's face. Something crosses his expression. A recognition. A longing. A tenderness.

It unsettles me.

Next I bring up a photo of Tyler and Luca, their arms around each other, grinning.

Whatever recognition or tenderness was there on Carl's face fades to indifference.

It pisses me off.

How dare he be indifferent about Tyler.

With a shove away, I stand up. I pace a circle around Carl, staring down at his duct-taped body. He doesn't respond to violence. He doesn't respond to questions. He doesn't respond to the darkness of this room when I close him in. He didn't respond to my threat to beat his wife. He hasn't even asked for food or water.

The only thing he's responded to is this picture of Randy.

My phone rings. It's Sheriff Owens. I close Carl up in the room and take the call.

He says, "Donna Kemp reported Carl missing. Know anything about that?"

"Can't say that I do."

GRACE IS SITTING at my front door when I pull into the driveway. She watches me through stony eyes as I climb from Grandpa's truck and walk to her.

"Where's Mom?" I ask.

"At my house."

"Sheriff Owens came by. Wanted to know if we'd seen Carl Kemp. Apparently, he had chemo, ordered an Uber to take him home, and yet never showed."

"Huh."

"There's a Dollar Store across from my dad's old studio. I know the girl who works the register. She said she's seen you going in and out of the studio." Grace levels me with a hard look. "What is going on, Nell?"

Through the dark, Mom walks toward us, coming from the direction of the pass-through. She looks exhausted. Like she's aged ten years in a few days. "Whatever you're doing at that studio, I want to see."

GRACE STANDS IN SHOCK, staring at Carl, his weak body duct taped and beaten. The flashlight I turned on isn't helping. It's flickering, casting Carl in an eerie, choppy pale glow.

He trembles.

I glower.

Mom stands beside me, showing none of Grace's shock. No, desperate hope is all over her face.

"He was singing their song," I tell them.

"Because he heard them in our front yard!" Grace exclaims. "That doesn't mean he took them."

I bring up the photo of Randy. "This is the little boy who went missing nearly eleven years ago. He knows this boy. He responded to this picture. He threatened me, saying I didn't know who I was dealing with and calling me a silly girl. He laughs and sneers. He said no matter what I did, he wouldn't cave. Why would he say that, huh?"

Grace just stares at me, her jaw open. "But he hasn't admitted to taking them?"

I don't respond because Grace doesn't get it.

Showing no fear, Mom kneels beside him. She cocks her head, really studying him. "Do you have children, Mr. Kemp?"

He nods.

"No, he doesn't," I say. "They're both dead."

"Is that why you took our boys?" she asks. "To replace yours?"

Holy shit, I hadn't thought of it from that angle.

"Are you worried your wife will be left alone? Is that what it is?"

Carl starts to come to life a little, looking up into Mom's face. He's responding to her gentleness.

"It's not too late," Mom says. "Think about how much pain you went through when you lost your children. Would you wish that on anybody? Those boys have mothers.

Mothers who miss them very much and want them back. Please." Her voice cracks, and she stops.

Carl's mouth moves.

She stares at his lips.

He spits right in her face.

For a second, Mom doesn't do anything, then she rears back and slaps him hard.

He chuckles. "Great green globs of greasy grimy gofer guts…"

Mom sobs.

"Stupid, stupid cunts." He laughs. "Good luck finding them."

"Oh my God," Grace whispers. "This is not happening."

"You believe me now?" I jab a finger in his direction. "Carl Kemp took Tyler and Luca. He knows where they are."

AFTER I GET MOM HOME, a sleeping pill down her, and settled in bed, I put a frozen meal in the microwave. While I watch it spin and begin to bubble, I make myself think.

Grandpa used to say he solved the best cases when he stopped moving and took time to look at details he wasn't currently fixated on. Currently, I'm fixated on Carl Kemp.

It's not in my nature to do what Grandpa said. I'm an action-oriented person. But I stand here, staring at my chicken marsala, and force myself to look at other things.

Like that man I saw standing in our yard. Why did he seem familiar?

And what about Randy from next door? Why come

back to the scene of the crime ten years later and take not one, but two more boys? What is it about this neighborhood?

Mom's words trickle in next. *Is that why you took our boys? To replace yours?*

The Kemp property was thoroughly searched. The boys aren't there. Do the Kemp's own other properties? Surely Sheriff Owens has already looked into that. It's not like I can call and ask, though. But I can do a property search.

The microwave dings. I open the door. Steam rolls out.

As I let it cool, I do a property search for Carl Kemp and get back one result—the trailer and an acre of land. Same comes up for Donna Kemp.

My phone rings. It's Grace.

She says, "You need to let Carl go."

"You don't believe he's guilty?"

"I didn't say that, but this isn't the way. Talk to Sheriff Owens. He'll understand."

A laugh erupts from me. "You've got to be kidding me. He will arrest me and put me in jail. He won't 'understand.'"

"You're going to kill him, Nell."

He's dying anyway, I want to say but don't. "No, I won't. I know his limit."

"Are you out of your mind?"

Not normally, no. But I have become someone different over the last few days.

"What if I tip Owens off? I won't tell him it's you. I'll tell him I found Carl like that."

I sigh. "Okay, then what?"

"Well, I don't know. I'll tell the sheriff everything Carl said. Then he can take it from there."

"You know what, I can't stop you. If that's what you want to do. Do it." I hang up.

I eat my microwave meal.

Grace calls back. "Fine. You do what you think you need to do. When the police find out he's there, I'll deny everything." With that, she clicks off.

TEN

A scream rattles me awake.

I'm out of bed and into Mom's room in no time.

She clings to me. "I had a horrible nightmare."

I stroke her hair. "Sh, it's okay."

"I heard him. I saw him. I smelled him."

"I know."

"He was locked in the shed." Mom cries.

I continue stroking her hair.

She pushes me off of her and jumps from bed. "The shed! We've never checked the shed!"

She rushes from the house out into a just dawning morning. Without putting on a coat or shoes, she runs in socks across the wet ground. She treads a path down the side of the house into the backyard. At the shed, she yanks the lock.

"Why is this locked?" She yanks harder. "Why is this locked? Tyler? Tyler, you in there? Where's the key? WHERE'S THE KEY?"

"Mom, Tyler's not in there." I come up behind her.

She yanks even harder. The shed vibrates. "Open this.

Get this open now. Please. Please. Please!" She falls to the ground, sobbing. *"Please."* She grabs me. "Make Carl talk. *Please.*"

I GOT MOM BACK INSIDE, into the tub, and then changed into dry clothes.

Now she sits in the living room, dazed, staring at the wall.

And I stand outside, studying the shed. In all my many visits here to see Grandpa, I've never once seen inside this shed. He told me he had surplus hunting supplies in it, and I never doubted that.

Why am I now?

In my hand, I hold the key ring I found in the kitchen drawer. I choose the one labeled "shed" and fit it into the padlock. I turn it. The lock pops open.

The door swings out and with it, a musty scent of stale closed-up air. Though it's daylight out, I still flip on a flashlight. It illuminates metal shelves filled with MRE meals, neatly folded clothes, ammunition, rope, tools, knives, gun cases, cardboard boxes with no label, and a large bag of used lye.

A carved wooden box on the top shelf catches my eye. Small and rectangular, the polished mahogany glints in my flashlight beam. Only a latch holds it in place, and when I take it down, I discover the shape of a heart neatly burned into the top. I open the latch and inside rests an old-fashioned key, it too with a heart etched into it.

I could be wrong, but I'm pretty sure I've seen this key before.

FROZEN RAIN COMES DOWN. Hitting the wipers, I squint through the windshield. The Dollar Store comes into view. I pull in and park, and with a stifled yawn, I run through the sleet.

Inside, I buy a Mountain Dew.

"Not much of a breakfast," she says.

"Believe me, I wouldn't drink this crap unless I was in dire need." I pay for the drink, unscrew the lid, and gulp some down.

The TV behind the counter shows two police boats on a nearby rock quarry with divers deployed. Search and rescue dogs roam the woods surrounding the quarry. A ticker at the bottom says they're looking for the missing boys.

She notices what has my attention. "Want me to turn it off?"

"No, I'm glad to see it. Catch you later." I trudge across the parking lot back out to the truck. For a second I sit with the heat on, drinking more sugar and caffeine, staring across the street at the abandoned studio.

If the girl who works here saw me going in and out of that building, who else has?

I hope Carl froze during the night. Maybe the promise of heat will make him talk. Or...food. I glance around, trying to remember if there are any fast-food restaurants near here and that's when I see him—Sheriff Owens.

He sits in his car, parked down the road.

"Shit." I grimace.

He's following me. And if I hadn't glanced up, I wouldn't have seen him.

Think, Nell, think.

I put the truck in reverse and drive home. For the

second time in the last few days, the sheriff follows me the whole way.

I don't go in the house. I confront him. "Don't you have better things to do like search for my brother?"

"Why were you in that part of town?"

"I heard there was a search going on at the quarry. I swung by." That's plausible as the Dollar Store would be on my way home from the quarry.

He stares into my eyes, looking for traces of a lie. He must see sadness instead because something shifts in his expression, becoming gentle.

"Tyler's going to need you and your mom when he comes home," he says. "You two need to take care of each other."

For some reason, his gentle tone grates my nerves. I look away. "Kids that are gone more than a week have half a chance of being found. Give it a month and little to no chance at all. Not alive, at least."

"It hasn't been a week yet."

"That's not a good response."

I OPEN *my eyes to see Tyler standing beside Grandpa's couch. I try to speak. I try to touch him, but I'm too shocked to move. He holds out an old-fashioned key with a heart etched into it.*

My body jolts awake. I jack knife up off the couch. My eyes tear. I reach for my little brother, but of course, he's not there.

It's been hours since Owens followed me home. I sat down here, waiting for enough time to transpire before I could leave again. I must have dozed off.

Still dressed in my bomber jacket, I stare at the spot where Tyler just stood in my dream.

My face hardens.

I'm out of the house and around to the shed in seconds. I throw open the door and I stare intently at the contents. I'd put the wood box with the engraved heart back up on the shelf, but I take it down now and open it up.

Dressed in pajama bottoms, crocs, and an oversized sweatshirt, Mom quietly approaches. She holds a cup of coffee between her gloved hands. When I look into her face, her expression shows curiosity, and fright.

"Mom, what does this key go to?"

She steps inside the shed. "I've never seen inside of this. Ever." Placing her coffee on a dusty shelf, she drags an unmarked cardboard box down. She holds it in her arms while she wedges off the lid. Inside are thick files. The tabs read first names only:

Bernard. Danny. Gerry. Kevin. Max. Peter. Randy. Sean. Thomas. Wade.

Ten total. All boys.

Her gloved finger tabs through them. She looks over at me with baffled, wide eyes. I choose the first one "Bernard" and slide it from the box. My heart picks up pace as I open it.

The top page shows a picture of a little boy with MISSING written across the border in red. It dates back forty years. If I remember correctly, that's when Grandpa left the Army and became a cop. The next sheet gives stats: height, weight, address, social security, parents' names, and siblings. After that comes witness statements, details on neighbors, and a timeline. After that are pictures of Bernard's home, belongings, school, playground, and family members. There are pages of notes Grandpa took on the investigation to find the little boy. I note the address where Bernard lived. I think that's one county over.

Quickly, I thumb through the rest of the pages, dreading that I'll find something I don't want to—though I'm not sure what. But I see only more details of a thorough investigation.

Or a thorough cover-up.

I don't like that I just had that thought.

Mom's looking at the one labeled "Danny." She shivers. "What the hell is this?"

I don't answer. Because I'm not sure if it is an investigation or a cover-up. I'm not sure about Grandpa at all anymore.

She hands the box to me. "I don't want to look at those."

ELEVEN

I don't take my usual route getting to the studio and I don't park in the rear of the building. No, I park several blocks away, taking the long way, cutting through the parking lot of another deserted building, frozen trees, and coming up on the backside.

The good thing about the studio is that it sits in a part of town where many more deserted buildings are. Really the Dollar Store is the only place still in business around here.

Safely inside, I stare at the files spread out on the studio floor. Carl's in the corner, quietly observing me. I've been here for hours, searching for a connection, but all I feel is even more perplexed.

If I was hoping to uncover secrets, it's not working.

For forty years, little boys have gone missing, all within a ninety-mile radius of White Quail, Tennessee. Grandpa's name is listed on all the cases, the earliest one as an assistant and then as lead investigator on the rest. All were unsolved. Sheriff Owens' name pops up in a few of the later files after he joined the force.

Are these files Grandpa's ghosts? Are they reminders of how he could have done better? Or are they a window into something darker?

I don't know, but I'm currently looking at the one labeled "Randy." Of all the boys, Randy was the closest one, geographically, to Grandpa. I imagine this one plagued Grandpa more than the others. This one happened right next door.

"He's a good boy," Carl whispers.

I freeze.

"Who? Randy?" I show him the photo. "What do you mean he's a good boy? Present tense as in he's still alive?"

His eyes tear. "I'm dying."

"Oh, stop the bullshit. I don't feel sorry for you."

"I need to go home. I need to say bye."

"Tell me where Tyler and Luca are, and sure, you can go."

He opens his mouth, and he screams. It's so loud, I flinch. He thrashes, rolling his body back and forth, getting enough momentum that he bowls himself right over the files and into me. I shove him hard. He rolls back into the corner.

"You want this to stop? Tell me where the boys are."

More screaming.

"WHERE?"

Screaming. Horrible, horrible screaming.

I take a breath, gathering the files. Carl thrashes, knocking his head over and over again into the dirty rubberized floor. "Stop it."

He keeps going.

"Stop it! You're going to hurt yourself."

He keeps going.

"STOP IT!" I lunge across just as his body stills. I roll

him over, seeing fresh blood. I feel for a pulse, finding a steady one. He knocked himself out.

"You stupid idiot," I mutter, surprised at the tears in my voice. "Why did you do that?"

TWELVE

An hour later I stare deliriously at Grandpa's files while Carl stares deliriously at me. I want to throw the files across the room, but I make myself breathe, and think. A notepad is balanced on my knee. I begin jotting notes:

- *40 years ago, the first child was abducted.*
- *What's the abductor's motivation?*
- *Ten boys total, random timeline.*
- *None recovered.*
- *All middle-class, Caucasian families.*
- *Last one taken ten years ago, Randy McMillan.*
- *Why take two more boys now?*

My pencil taps that last question. I think of Mom's comment about replacing Carl's dead sons.

Not too long ago I began reading a criminology book. There were detailed cases of abductions, specifically one about a teenage girl who was taken at a young age and grew up thinking her abductor was her real parent.

What am I suggesting here? That Carl is taking little boys and keeping them? If that's the case, where are they?

I think of the photos that I saw of Carl and Donna's two boys, both dead.

Or are they?

I pick up Randy's picture, scrutinizing the eyes and lines of his face. Something about him seems familiar, just like when I saw that man at my house. Something about him seemed familiar as well. Are they the two sons in the photo?

If that's the case then Donna lied about the older one committing suicide because I saw him. I just didn't realize who it was.

Or maybe I'm reaching here. I'm looking for something that's not there.

Carl starts to cry.

It only serves to irritate me.

The door to the soundproof room swings open.

My heart lurches to my throat. "Mom," I breathe. "How did you get here?"

"Uber."

"You took an Uber? Jesus Christ."

"I had the driver drop me off a couple of blocks away. I'm not stupid."

"I didn't say you were."

She takes a slow step in, peering at Carl. "I don't suppose he's said anything."

"Nothing of use."

"You started this, ya know. You're the one who took him. You got Grace involved. Me, too. You're going to go to jail for this if we don't figure him out."

Icy prickles ting my skin. "What do you mean 'figure him out?'"

"What do you think is going to happen? Tyler's not coming back. He's gone." Her voice cracks. "My baby's gone." She falls to her knees, sobbing. "This has to stop." Mom wipes the tears from her face, trying in vain to calm herself. "It has to."

"Mom, don't give up."

"Let's take care of him before someone finds him. We'll dump his body somewhere. I don't know where. We'll bleach this place. Or hell, let's burn it down."

"Mom..." I crawl over the files and across the floor. She begins sobbing again, and I hold her. "Let me take you home."

A scratched whisper floats across the air. "They're dead."

I freeze.

Mom yanks away from me. "What did he say?"

"Nothing. He's messing with you. Don't listen to him."

Trembling, Mom's breath quickens. Tension builds in her to an excruciating level that has her visibly shaking.

He giggles.

"You mother fucker, shut up!"

Another giggle, this one slower. The sound enrages me. Abrupt darkness moves in on me. Jabbing. Prodding. Swallowing me whole.

I want to hurt him. Badly.

I breathe—in, out, in. But it's not me who screams and launches herself at Carl. It's Mom.

"You son of a bitch! YOU SON OF A BITCH!" she yells.

Lunging to my feet, I pull her off of him. She whirls on me and smacks me across the face. "You were supposed to be watching Tyler! Why weren't you watching him?"

I'm so shocked, I don't respond. She's never hit me before.

She gives me a hateful look, before bursting into tears and rushing from the room.

I listen to the back door open, then slam shut. I listen to her crank the truck's engine. I listen to the tires squeal.

I keep standing, half expecting her to come back.

But she doesn't.

When I turn back to Carl, I see him staring at the photo of Randy McMillan.

"Do you want to go home?" I ask.

Carl's swollen and bruised head rotates toward me. He whimpers.

"Is that a yes?"

He screams.

Calmly, I gather the files.

He thrashes, his screams turning to screeches.

I put the files into the box. I look at him, and I scream just as loudly.

His body curls and uncurls, fighting against the duct tape wrapped tightly around him. Baring his teeth, he hisses.

I hiss back.

Carl goes ballistic, trying to break free.

"Good luck with that. You're not getting out until I want you to."

He rolls across the floor, leaving a smear of bodily fluid in his wake. I yank him back, towering over him, my fists clenched, staring down into his cadaver-like face.

"You'll never find them," he spits. "*Never.*"

THIRTEEN

From the studio, I walk home.

Mom haphazardly parked the truck in the yard with the keys still in the ignition. I get in and drive straight to Donna Kemp.

Her rental car is parked where it was before. I march right past it and up to the front door.

I don't knock. I turn the knob and let myself in.

I hear the shower running in the back of the house.

I go from room to room, opening doors, finding nothing.

In the living room, I pick up the one photo of their youngest son. On my phone, I bring up four-year-old Randy. Granted, years have passed, but their "late in life" baby "Harry" is Randy McMillan. Dead, according to Donna, in a hunting accident.

Next, I look at their older son. I knew the man standing outside my home seemed familiar. That's him. The one who supposedly committed suicide. Is he another kidnapped boy, grown now? Or is he a true son?

I put the picture down. Beside it is a shallow dish with

trinkets—earrings, sewing supplies, a letter opener, and an old-fashioned key.

Son of a bitch.

I pick it up. It's the same one I found in Grandpa's shed, down to the color and weight, design, and even the goddamn heart etched into it. With it in my hand, I turn to see Donna standing in the doorway, dressed in a robe, a gun pointed at me.

"Where are they?" I demand.

She steps aside, motioning me into the kitchen. "Let's have some tea."

"I don't want any tea."

Donna moves into the kitchen, getting tea from a cabinet and two cups. She turns on the faucet and fills the kettle. The stove clicks as she lights it. All the time she keeps the gun and one eye on me. She notes the key that I hold and smiles lovingly.

"You remind me of your grandfather. It's the eyes. Determined. Suspicious."

FOURTEEN

Jill told the Uber driver to drop her off a block from the studio. She got out, taking the oversized purse with her.

She pulled the hoodie over her head and walked quickly to her destination.

At the rear of the studio, she took the mini bolt cutters from the oversized bag and snapped the lock on the back door. It easily slipped free, falling to the cracked pavement.

Jill stepped inside. No sound could be heard.

She walked through the gutted building to the black door that separated her from Carl. She opened it, finding him moving around, moaning and shaking.

Jill stood in the doorway. From her oversized purse, she took a mini-flashlight and flicked it on. She looked around, noting the stains of urine and blood smeared across the interior. Carl thumped his head on the floor. Jill put the purse down. She extracted a bag full of her father's pills that she found in the bathroom.

Carl stopped moving.

"I'm not doing this for you, believe me. I'm doing this for Nell. I won't let her go down for this." She took out a handful of pills, showing them to Carl. "Are they really dead?"

Carl nodded.

"Just tell me why, and it'll be a peaceful ending for you."

Carl frowned.

Jill stepped closer. "Why did you take them?"

Carl's frown deepened.

Jill waited, not nervous. More, at peace with her decision.

His lips moved. "They were being bad boys, and bad boys need to learn lessons."

She nodded, relieved to hear him speak. "And where did you take them?"

"I put them in the hole."

Jill felt the color drain from her face. She closed her eyes. Her breathing got away from her. "Did they feel pain?"

"Yes."

Her eyes opened back up. She shined the light on Carl's face. "How many times have you done this?"

"A lot. I like teaching lessons. I kept one, though, because he was my favorite. I named him Harry after my dad."

"What was his name before Harry?"

"Randy."

"Where is Randy now?"

"Gone, but always alive in my mind. Would you like to know how I killed the boys?"

Jill barely breathed.

"I hit them over and over again, just like my father used to hit me."

Jill remained silent.

"I want to die. That's why you're here, right? To do what your daughter couldn't?"

Numbly Jill nodded. She barely registered walking over and pouring the pills into his mouth. She barely registered him swallowing them.

Just stay calm, Dad used to tell the crazies.

Jill told herself that now as Carl opened his mouth, wanting more. And she gave them to him.

Carl swallowed. She waited for him to ask for more, but he didn't. Instead, he smiled and closed his eyes.

Jill sat beside him, tears streaming down her face. She wasn't sure how long she sat there, watching Carl die. She should be horrified at what she'd done. Yet she wasn't.

"Oh my God, Jill."

She didn't have to turn around to know Sheriff Owens stood behind her.

FIFTEEN

"Just give me Tyler and Luca. I don't care what you do. Run. Hide. I don't care. Just give me the boys."

Donna chuckles. "Good God, you *are* just like your grandfather. He said the exact same thing when he found out. 'Run,' he said. 'I know this isn't on you. Just let me give all the families peace.' Except it *was* on me. I knew what my husband was doing. It's why I carried on my oh-so-secret love affair with your grandfather. It was the only way to keep the law on my side."

"Using the key with the heart?"

"Yes, he bought a 'love bungalow' as your grandfather used to call it. Even put it in my maiden name in case something happened to him. Such a sentimental man." Fondly, she smiles.

Then the smile fades, and her eyes don't waver. The gun in her hand doesn't shake. She has no fear as she considers me. "Do you have a weapon?"

"Like I would tell you if I did."

"Don't talk back to me, girl. I promise you, you will regret it."

"No, I don't have a weapon."

"Not too bright coming here with nothing to use. You underestimated an old woman." The kettle whistles. She steps aside, motioning me out of the living room and back into the kitchen. "Pour the water into the mug on the right."

I walk across the floor, my brain spinning.

A round table sits in the center of the kitchen with a throw rug underneath. I circle it, coming to a stop at the stove. I turn the burner off and pour the hot water into the cup on the right. I note something ground up at the bottom.

Something poisonous, I'm sure.

"I have your husband," I say. "I'll let him go if you give me the boys."

"Where is he?"

"Doesn't work that way. Give me Tyler and Luca. I give you Carl."

She doesn't respond.

I turn to look at her, pleased to see that my words have rattled her. "I saw your son—Junior. The one you claimed committed suicide. He's very much alive."

"Junior's more insurance. He was your grandfather's, only I kept that tight to my chest to be used if needed."

"Your husband didn't know?"

"Carl always knew about the affair. He understood I had to do it to protect his proclivities. He never knew about Junior's true DNA. Ten years ago, I told Carl in the heat of an argument. He banished Junior from our lives, and I haven't seen him since. How did he look, healthy?"

"Yes."

"Well anyway, that's how Carl ended up taking Randy. He was parked outside your grandfather's place, seething. He saw Randy and ended up taking him instead. He didn't plan on keeping Randy. But he fell in love with that boy. It was a love he never held for Junior. Randy was the son he always wanted. 'Harry' became ours."

"Were you lying about him dying?"

"Unfortunately, Harry is gone."

"When did my grandfather find out about Junior?"

"Six months ago, right before he died."

"Why Tyler and Luca?"

"Carl was grieving Harry. He's been driving by his old house pretty much every single day, reminiscing. He saw Tyler and Luca and I don't know, maybe he wanted another Harry, maybe he wanted one last hoorah before he died, or maybe he wanted to make sure I wouldn't be alone. Whatever it was, he brought them home."

She nods to the cup. "Should be cool enough now."

I take a breath, looking at the brown water.

"Ground cherry pits. It takes a while. You're a tall girl but not as tall as your grandfather. It took hours for him. He left our 'love bungalow' and went home. You were visiting that weekend. He'd just confronted me with all the evidence. I told him Junior was his. He was so upset. Yet he still gave me the 'pack and run' speech. He was coming here the next day with a team to arrest Carl and look for the remains. None of that worked for me, though. He underestimated my loyalty to Carl."

"You killed my grandfather."

"I did." She nods to the cup. "Now, drink."

"No."

"Drink it or I will end your life right here in this kitchen right now. I'll get your brother and make him chop you up into little pieces."

"Where is he?"

"One. Two. Th—"

Trembling, I grab the tea. I drink, my eyes on her the

whole time. With half of it gone, I place it back on the counter.

"Let me see."

I open my mouth.

"Good girl. And don't worry, I didn't use ground pits on the boys. I have my own personal recipe for them. Keeps them nice and loopy. Now, put the keys to your grandfather's truck on the kitchen counter."

With shaky hands, I pull them from my front jeans pocket and place them in sight.

Donna motions me out, and I exit the house. She follows, the gun trained on my head. She directs me across the yard, down the driveway, across the road, and up to the abandoned shack.

"My father used to live here. House is still in his name. God rest his soul. I'll never forget Carl's face the first time he took a boy. It's been fifty years ago now before we even moved to this area. I can't remember the boy's name, but he was being a bad boy to his mommy. Talking back to her at the park. My husband wanted to teach him a lesson. He never had the patience for bratty kids. He believed in corporal punishment, as do I. So did your grandfather, you know. I think that's why we got along so well."

She stops at the front door. "'They mooned me.' That's what he said when he brought them here, dropped them off, then headed right back out. You found him later that night, parked at that gas station." She hands me the key. "'He stuck his tongue out at me.' That's what he said when he brought Randy home." Donna chuckles. "It was always something with Carl."

She nods for me to unlock the door.

My pulse ratchets up as I step into a dark room, lit only by the daylight filtering in the door. The one board I removed from the window has been nailed back in place. I see the same things I saw before—a woven rope rug, a wooden ladder, and a wood burning stove.

"Tyler! Luca!"

"Turn around."

I do.

Rearing back, she punches me hard with her fist. My head snaps to the right. My ears ring.

Donna keeps the gun trained on me. "Move the rug."

I do, revealing a large piece of plywood. The tea kicks in quicker than I expected, making me teeter.

"Move it out of the way."

The smell of ammonia hits me, and I wince. My eyes water as I stare down into a grave-like hole in the ground, maybe seven feet deep. She fires a shot into my thigh.

I stumble. The soil crumbles out from under me and I fall into the pit. I land hard, blood bubbling from the wound. That's when I see Tyler, huddled in the dirt, dressed only in his underwear and covered in welts.

"Tyler!" I scramble over and check for a pulse, finding a thread of one. I kiss his face. "I'm here. I love you. I'm here."

Donna starts to pull the plywood back over the hole. "That one you can have. I'm keeping the other. He's going to be my new Harry."

"Where is he?"

"Under the kitchen floor in our storm cellar. Luca was here in the hole—they both were—when the cops searched our place." She tosses a lighter in. "Luca and I will be long gone when the sheriff comes back. There's lots to keep you two company down there. Look around. If you can manage to stem the bleeding you might last as long as twenty-four hours before the tea completely takes you."

She slides the plywood over the hole, blanketing us in darkness. I hear her leave the house.

I jab my finger down my throat and make myself throw up. I do it several times until only bile remains.

My thumb rolls across the lighter, bringing it to life. It flickers off of dirt walls. The area looks to be as long as it is deep—seven feet or so, roughly dug, with jabbing marks presumably from the shovel used to dig this hell hole. In the back corner, a chunky mound of dissolved and corrosive human remains leers at me. Despite having nothing left in my stomach, I heave more bile.

The flame dies.

SIXTEEN

Blood pulses from my thigh. In the darkness, I slide my belt from its loops and tighten it above the bullet hole. Carefully, I stand. Once again, I flick the lighter to life. I look at the underside of the plywood. I can break through that. I know I can. Stretching up, I estimate I need at least one more foot of height.

I move the light around the hole, illuminating rusted and moldy toys, a broken brick, a dirty kid's sneaker, Tyler, and bones. My head reels. I lose my breath.

The light goes out.

I try to breathe, but the ammonia burns my lungs and eyes.

My fingers dig into the dirt wall. I climb, making it a few inches before the dirt crumbles and I fall back down. How many little boys did just this? They desperately climbed, their tiny fingers digging in. They screamed. They cried. They died in fear.

My thumb rolls across the lighter, this time inspecting the walls further up. I spy a tree root looping and protruding near the top. Bingo. I jump and miss, landing hard on my leg. My breath hisses in.

I try again, jumping, and this time my hand grabs hold of the root. I pull myself up, my teeth gritted, and I punch the underside of the plywood. Nothing happens. My muscles shake. I punch again, and again nothing happens. I lose hold, falling and landing on my butt. Something jabs into my hip, and I grimace. It's the broken brick.

Fisting it, I make quick work of jumping and grabbing the root. With the brick, I punch the plywood, and I punch it again. Wood splinters, slivers hitting me in the face. I yank at a chunk, tossing it down into the hole.

With all my force, I punch again with the brick. The skin on my knuckles breaks as my fist meets the underside of the rug. Yes! I punch again, wincing. Blood smears the wood, but my hand and the brick once again go through. The hole widens. I yank at the plywood, breaking away a sizable chunk.

Then another.

And another.

The hole in the wood grows larger, enough for me to grab the rug and pull it down. I toss the brick out into the shack and use the thick rug as an aid in climbing out.

I roll to my back, struggling for breath, my heart racing. I don't know how much poison is in my system, but I have to act fast.

I grab the rickety wood ladder and lower it into the hole. Seconds later I have Tyler in my arms and I'm climbing back out. His weight is insignificant and reminds me of how tiny he is. How fragile. I hold him tight, kissing his dirty face.

Taking the brick with me, I go to the front door, finding it locked from the outside. With the brick, I hammer away at the lock. Over and over and over again. It takes all my energy and focus, but the lock breaks free.

I'm out with Tyler, stumbling through the morning hours, down the gravel driveway, and across onto the Kemp property.

Grandpa's truck is gone. I note a rough cut path in the woods she likely drove it down to hide it. Her rental car is still here though.

My body sways as I stare at the trailer now just a few yards away. Carefully, I scrutinize the windows, but I don't see movement.

With the brick still in my hand and Tyler still in my arms, I approach the door. The inside greets me, overly warm and filled with that incessant ticking clock. The tea I drank still sits on the counter.

The room spins, and I have to grab onto the counter to steady myself.

When I regain equilibrium, I place Tyler on the floor and hurry over to the kitchen table. I push it to the side and throw back the rug. A square hatch-like door covers the storm cellar where Luca is. One single barrel bolt secures it.

The bolt releases. I open the hatch, placing it to the side. Wide steps lead down into a small cellar.

That's where I see Luca, fully clothed, curled in the fetal position, his breaths shallow. My heart contracts. I rush over to him, feeling for a pulse and finding a not-so-steady one. Tears push my eyes as I gather him into my arms. "It's me, Luca. I've got you."

Like Tyler, his weight is nothing, but my arm muscles tremble. I hold him tight, making my way out of the cellar and back into the kitchen. The room warps. *Hang on, Nell. Hang on.*

The sound of shuffling feet snaps me back. I turn just as

a shadow shifts. I register it right as something slams into my face. I stumble back, losing my grip on Luca. He slides from my arms and I'm just aware enough to break his fall. My vision blurs. I blink hard. Donna's face distorts.

With a scream, I blindly launch myself at her. The brick is next to the hatch. I pick it up, and I don't think. I act.

I punch her with it.

Over.

And over.

And over again.

I punch her until she stops moving.

Until she stops breathing.

Until her blood soaks both of us.

Panting, I roll off of her. Blood pulses from my thigh. I try to re-buckle the belt, but darkness moves in.

I reach for the boys. My fingers touch Tyler's back, and then my whole world goes black.

SEVENTEEN

My lashes flutter open. My bandaged and elevated leg is the first thing I see. Sheriff Owens is the second. He sits in a chair beside my hospital bed.

"Hello," he says.

"Where's my brother?" I try to sit up.

"Tyler's safe and well. So is Luca. You're in a hospital."

A window behind him shows another winter storm moving in. "What time is it? How long have I been out?"

"It's one in the afternoon on Saturday. You had surgery to remove the bullet in your thigh. You also have a broken nose. Not to mention the poison that was in your system. I've been here a few minutes. I wanted to be the first one to speak with you."

"Across from the Kemp place is an abandoned house. There's a hole in the ground with remains. Carl is—"

Carl. Shit.

Shit. Shit. Shit.

"Where's Mom?" I try to get up again.

The sheriff stands. "Stay still."

"But—"

"I know everything."

I'm not sure he does, so I remain quiet.

Even though the door is closed, he lowers his voice. "Carl Kemp is dead."

He was alive the last time I saw him.

"Your mother tortured and killed him for infor—"

"No, she did—"

He holds a hand up. "Yes, she did. That is her story and that is the one she is insisting on. Do you understand me? You are all Tyler has left. We know Carl kidnapped Luca and Tyler and so many others. Forensics is out at that abandoned house now excavating the place for remains, though with the lye treatment in the hole, it's going to take time. I knew your grandfather and Donna Kemp were having an affair. I also know those missing boys haunted him. I worked on a few of the cases with him. I'm glad he's not alive to know Donna and her husband were the abductors."

He knew.

"We also know their one son Harry was actually Randy McMillan. We assume their other son Junior was also one of the missing boys. Or perhaps he was Donna and Carl's real son. Did Donna give any indication on that?"

With a hand steadier than expected, I reach for the water on my side table. After several long swallows, I hold it in my lap. "No, she didn't say."

"Hm." He doesn't believe me.

That's okay. Though Grandpa had his faults, the secret of him being Junior's father is safe with me.

The door opens and in walks a nurse pushing Tyler in a wheelchair. Remnants of shock cloud his eyes. He tries to smile, but the effort falls from his lips.

I smile. "Hi, Tyler."

His voice comes withered and shaky. "Hi."

"He's doing good," the nurse says. "He wanted to see you."

My brother stares at me, unable to speak, almost like I'm an apparition versus his sister. There's a darkness in his eyes that unsettles me.

To me only, Sheriff Owens whispers, "I will do everything in my power for your mom. You are all Tyler has now. Remember that."

EIGHTEEN

One Year Later

A female security guard presses a button, and the door to the courtyard swings open. Tyler slowly walks beside me, earbuds in, over to greet Mom. Gently, she hugs him and kisses his head.

With a pleasant smile, she reaches out an arm for me.

Once a month, Mom's facility does a family day with boxed lunches, games, and puppets. The patients with ninety days of good behavior are allowed to attend if a family member agrees to come, too.

We never miss one.

After we say hello, we sit beside each other at a picnic table. Tyler stays tight against me, listening to his music.

It's been a hard year for all of us, Tyler the most. He barely speaks. He's yet to tell anybody what happened during that week a year ago. Luca seems adjusted, but he too does not speak of that week. The one thing that troubles me is that they don't want to be around each other anymore. The child psychiatrist that Tyler sees says it's post traumatic stress in that they remind each other of the time they were held captive.

Mom reaches across the picnic table and touches Tyler's arm. He slides it out of the way, tucking it tight to his body. Calmly, she smiles, not taking offense. He turns his music up.

"How are you?" I ask her.

"Good. I'm on kitchen duty for the next thirty days. I like the girls in there. Should be okay. Owens says you snagged a spot on a task force. That's amazing! I'm proud of you."

"He pulled strings."

"Doesn't matter. You deserve it."

Truth is, I wavered on the decision to follow in my grandfather's footsteps, and in the end, decided yes. I graduated from the academy six months ago and have officially been on the job for an equal amount of time. I like it more than I imagined I would.

I want to be the one who doesn't let things slide through the cracks. I *will* make a difference.

Mom says, "He visits me, you know."

"I know." Because of yet more strings Sheriff Owens pulled, Mom's second-degree murder charge got her placed in a mental hospital versus prison.

"And night classes?" she asks. "Going okay?"

"Yes, but at this rate I'll be your age when I graduate."

"Nah, it'll go by quicker than you think." Straightening her back, she takes my hand, seemingly possessed by newfound strength. She's like that every time I visit her. "Nell, you need to come to terms with me being here."

I nod, because I know she needs me to be strong.

"How is Grace?" she asks, changing the subject. "The last time you were here you said she was struggling with her part of things. What we did, we had to for the boys. Grace knows that. I know that. *You* should know that, too."

"Grace is getting there. We talk nearly every day. Wedding plans are keeping her focused on something else."

"Because of you, Tyler and Luca are alive."

Again, I nod. But I will always regret she's locked in here for something I put in motion. I will also always respect her and admire her for this selfless act. "You're not fragile. Do you know that?"

"What are you talking about?"

"Grandpa told me that. He told me you were fragile and that I needed to take care of you. He was wrong." I squeeze her hand.

We fall silent after that, staring at each other. I want to tell her that she has a half brother, but I keep that to myself. Perhaps one day he'll show up again. If he does, I have a hell of a lot of questions for him. Did he know what Carl was doing? I'd like to think not. But he grew up under their roof. He had to at least suspect. Plus, where did he think "Harry" came from? Perhaps Donna weaved some adoption tale.

Finally, though, I ask the question that has weighed heavy on me since speaking with Nancy McMillan. "Mom, did Grandpa abuse you?"

To my surprise, she doesn't break eye contact with me. "Why would you ask me that?"

"Did he?"

"Your grandpa was a complicated man. He sure loved you, though."

Even though I suspected what her answer would be, disbelief still courses through me, followed quickly by intense love. This woman in front of me is strong and brave.

In this careful moment, so much about her makes sense now. I spent a lifetime loving her, but not respecting her as I should. I never bothered to understand her. I only ever questioned her. Early on I became her parent. I never allowed her to be mine.

I wanted to grow up and be just like Grandpa.

Now, I want to honor and emulate my mother.

"I love you. I'm so sorry Grandma left you alone with him. I love you so very much, Mom. I hope you know that."

"I never wanted you to know. He did love you most."

"I don't care. My loyalty is to you. Always."

I look into her teary eyes. Her mouth wobbles with a happy smile.

On the table sits three box lunches. We open them and begin eating.

It's not a perfect life, but it's a good one.

It's *our* life, and I will cherish every moment of it.

BOOKS BY S. E. GREEN

Nell Brach Series:

Gone

Silence

Unseen

Other Books:

Before Then Now

Ten Years Later

The Family

Sister Sister

The Lady Next Door

The Strangler

The Suicide Killer

Monster

The Third Son

Vanquished

Mother May I

Printed in Dunstable, United Kingdom